Mark Twain
THE ADVENTURES
of TOM SAWYER

essay by
Andrew Jay Hoffman, PhD
Brown University

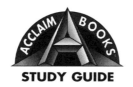

STUDY GUIDE

The Adventures of Tom Sawyer

adaptation by H. Miller
art by Aldo Rubano

Dale-Chall R.L.: 6.9

ISBN 1-57840-001-5

Acclaim Books, New York, NY
Printed in the United States

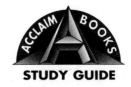

STUDY GUIDE

TOM SAWYER

DOWN IN THE GREAT SOUTHWEST EARLY IN THE 19TH CENTURY, IN THE TYPICAL AMERICAN VILLAGE OF ST. PETERSBURG, LIVED A TYPICAL AMERICAN BOY BY THE NAME OF TOM SAWYER. TOM BEING AN ORPHAN STAYED WITH HIS AUNT POLLY AND HIS STEP-BROTHER AND SISTER, SIDNEY AND MARY.

TOM WAS A RESTLESS AND ADVENTUROUS BOY AND AUNT POLLY HAD HER HANDS FULL KEEPING HER NEPHEW IN LINE; WHAT, WITH HIS PLAYING HOOKEY FROM SCHOOL AND GETTING HIMSELF ENMESHED IN ONE SCRAPE AFTER ANOTHER.

ONE DAY...

Aldo Rubano

TOM! OH TOM!

WHAT'S GONE WITH THAT BOY, I WONDER? YOU, TOM!

WELL, I LAY. IF I GET HOLD OF YOU, I'LL...

Y-O-U-U, TOM!

THERE! I MIGHT A' THOUGHT OF THAT CLOSET! WHAT HAVE YOU BEEN DOIN' THERE?

NOTHING, AUNT POLLY!

NOTHING! LOOK AT YOUR HANDS! AND LOOK AT YOUR MOUTH! WHAT IS THAT TRUCK?

I-I DON'T KNOW!

THEN, SIDNEY SPOKE UP...

WELL NOW, IF I DIDN'T THINK YOU SEWED HIS COLLAR WITH WHITE THREAD -- BUT IT'S BLACK!

BUT TOM DID NOT WAIT TO HEAR ANYMORE...

SIDDY, I'LL LICK YOU FOR THAT!

IN A SAFE PLACE...

SHE'D NEVER NOTICED IT IF IT HADN'T BEEN FOR SID! CONFOUND IT! SOMETIMES, SHE SEWS IT WITH WHITE THREAD --SOMETIMES WITH BLACK!

IN TWO MINUTES, HE FORGOT ALL HIS TROUBLES...

SUDDENLY, A STRANGER WAS BEFORE HIM...

WELL, WHAT A FANCY PANTS WE GOT HERE! THE SISSY'S ALL DRESSED UP IN HIS SUNDAY BEST AND HERE IT IS ONLY FRIDAY!

NEITHER BOY SPOKE, BUT KEPT EYEING EACH OTHER...

ON HIS WAY TO SCHOOL MONDAY, TOM MET HUCKLEBERRY FINN, THE VILLAGE BAD BOY. CHILDREN WERE STRICTLY FORBIDDEN TO SPEAK OR PLAY WITH HIM. THOSE CAUGHT DOING SO WERE SEVERELY PUNISHED, SO...

HELLO, HUCKY! WHAT'S THAT YOU GOT!

DEAD CAT!

LEMME SEE, HUCK! MY, HE'S PRETTY STIFF! WHERE'D YOU GET 'IM?

BOUGHT HIM OFF'N A BOY!

SAY, WHAT IS DEAD CATS GOOD FOR, HUCK?

GOOD FOR? WHY CURIN' WARTS WITH

I HEARD O' CURIN' WARTS WITH SPUNK WATER AND WITH BEANS...BUT I NEVER HEARD O' CURIN' 'EM WITH DEAD CATS!

WHY, THAT'S THE BEST WAY I KNOW OF! YOU TAKE YOUR CAT AND GO AND GET IN THE GRAVEYARD 'LONG ABOUT MIDNIGHT, WHEN SOMEBODY THAT WAS WICKED HAS BEEN BURIED...

AND WHEN IT'S MIDNIGHT, A DEVIL WILL COME AND WHEN THEY ARE TAKING THAT FELLER AWAY, YOU HEAVE YOUR CAT AFTER 'EM AND SAY, "DEVIL FOLLOW CORPSE, CAT FOLLOW DEVIL, WARTS FOLLOW CAT -- I'M DONE WITH YE!" THAT'LL FETCH ANY WART!

YES, AND YOU DONE MORE THAN THAT! FIVE YEARS AGO, YOU DROVE ME AWAY FROM YOUR FATHER'S KITCHEN AND I SWORE I'D GET EVEN WITH YOU! NOW, I'VE GOT YOU AND YOU GOT TO SETTLE!

THE DOCTOR STRUCK OUT SUDDENLY...

HERE, NOW, DON'T YOU HIT MY PARD!

AFTER A BITTER STRUGGLE THE DOCTOR SEIZED THE HEAVY HEADBOARD OF THE WILLIAMS GRAVE AND FELLED POTTER TO THE EARTH...

NOW'S MY CHANCE!

EEEEOW!

WHEN POTTER CAME TO, THE HALF-BREED ACCUSED HIM OF THE MURDER, BUT PROMISED NOT TO REVEAL THE SECRET...

A CASE O' COLD-BLOODED MURDER IF I EVER SAW ONE!

G'COME ON, HUCK W- WE SAW ENOUGH!

OH, JOE. I'LL BLESS YOU FOR THIS THE LONGEST DAY I LIVE!

COME ON, THIS AIN'T ANY TIME FOR BLUBBERIN'! MOVE ON AND DON'T LEAVE ANY TRACKS BEHIND YOU!

IF HE'S AS DRUNK AS HE LOOKS, HE WON'T THINK OF THE KNIFE TILL HE'S GONE SO FAR HE'LL BE AFRAID TO COME BACK FOR IT BY HIMSELF -- CHICKENHEART!

LATER, TOM AND HUCK, FEARFUL OF INJUN JOE'S VENGEANCE, VOWED NEVER TO REVEAL THEIR SECRET...

THERE IT IS, FINISHED! NOW, I'LL SHOW YOU HOW TO SIGN YOUR INITIALS HUCK!

THEIR PLEDGE WRITTEN IN THEIR OWN BLOOD...

HUCK FINN AND TOM SAWYER SWEARS THEY WILL KEEP MUM ABOUT THIS AND THEY WISH THEY MAY DROP DOWN DEAD IN THEIR TRACKS IF THEY EVER TELL AND ROT" T.S. H.F.

NEXT DAY, THE VILLAGE WAS ELECTRIFIED WITH THE GHASTLY NEWS. POTTER WAS SOON APPREHENDED AND THRUST INTO JAIL, OPENLY ACCUSED BY INJUN JOE OF THE MURDER...

TOM'S FEARFUL SECRET AND GNAWING CONSCIENCE DISTURBED HIS SLEEP FOR A WEEK...

TOM, YOU PITCH AROUND AND TOSS SO MUCH, YOU KEEP ME AWAKE HALF THE TIME!

THERE MUST BE SOMETHING ON YOUR MIND, TOM!

NOTHING! NOTHING'T I KNOW OF!

LAST NIGHT YOU SAID "IT'S BLOOD, IT'S BLOOD -- THAT'S WHAT IT IS!"

SUDDENLY, A REVEALING THOUGHT FLASHED THROUGH TOMS MIND!

BOYS, I KNOW WHO'S DROWNDED! IT'S US! THEY'RE LOOKIN' FOR US!

AT NIGHT, THE PIRATES RETURNED TO CAMP AND THE FERRYBOAT GAVE UP ITS SEARCH. THAT NIGHT, OVERCOME WITH AN IRRESISTABLE HOMESICKNESS, TOM WAITED UNTIL THE OTHERS HAD FALLEN ASLEEP..

THE NOTES I LEFT WILL EXPLAIN EVERYTHING!

A FEW MINUTES LATER, TOM WAS IN THE SHALLOW WATER, WADING TOWARDS THE SHORE...

SEVERAL HOURS LATER...

WHILLIKENS! THERE'S AUNT POLLY, JOE'S MOTHER AND SID AND MARY ACTIN' AS THO' SOME ONE HAD DIED!

THE LORD GIVETH AND THE LORD TAKETH AWAY! ONLY LAST SATURDAY MY JOE BUSTED A FIRECRACKER RIGHT UNDER MY NOSE! NOW, I'D HUG HIM AND BLESS HIM FOR IT!

POOR TOM WAS THE SAME WAY! BUT HE'S OUT OF HIS TROUBLES NOW! AND THE LAST WORDS I EVER HEARD HIM SAY...

I CAN'T STAND THEM CRYIN' ABOUT ME! I JUST CAN'T STAND IT!

MUFF POTTER WAS FINALLY BROUGHT TO TRIAL FOR THE MURDER OF DR. ROBINSON, WITH INJUN JOE AS THE STAR WITNESS. THEN CAME THE LAST MORNING OF THE TRIAL...

I KNOW JUST HOW YOU FEEL, TOM, BUT I'M AFEARED THER' AIN'T NOTHIN' WE CAN DO ABOUT IT!

HUCK, I FEEL JUST AWFUL!

SEVERAL WITNESSES WERE CALLED; THEIR TESTIMONY CLINCHED THE CERTAIN GUILT OF MUFF POTTER... SUDDENLY...

YOUR HONOR, I WISH TO CALL TOM SAWYER TO THE WITNESS STAND...

IMMEDIATELY, ALL EYES WERE UPON TOM AS HE TOOK HIS PLACE ON THE STAND...

THOMAS SAWYER, WHERE WERE YOU ON THE 17TH OF JUNE, ABOUT THE HOUR OF MIDNIGHT?

IN THE GRAVEYARD -- WITH A FRIEND AND A -- A DEAD CAT!

TELL THE COURT WHAT YOU SAW!

TREMBLING WITH EMOTION, TOM RELATED HIS HARROWING EXPERIENCES THAT NIGHT IN THE GRAVEYARD. FINALLY AS THE STRAIN OF THE PENT-UP EMOTION REACHED ITS CLIMAX...

TOM AND BECKY WERE SOON SEPARATED FROM THE OTHER CHILDREN...

I WONDER HOW LONG WE'VE BEEN DOWN HERE, TOM? WE'D BETTER START BACK!

YES, I RECKON WE BETTER! P'RAPS WE BETTER!

I HOPE WE WON'T GET LOST! IT WILL BE AWFUL!

SHUCKS! I'LL FIND THE WAY EASY ENOUGH!

I HOPE, THERE ARE SO MANY PASSAGES, I DON'T KNOW WHICH TO TAKE.

THEY SOON FOUND THEMSELVES LOST IN THE MAZE OF PASSAGES...

Y O-O-O T HERE!

Y O-O-O T HERE!

OH, DON'T DO IT AGAIN, TOM! THE ECHOES SOUND TOO HORRID!

IT IS HORRID, BUT I BETTER, BECKY! THEY MIGHT HEAR US, YOU KNOW!

SOON, TOM BLEW OUT BECKY'S CANDLE. SHE UNDERSTOOD AND HER HEART SANK, THEY MUST ECONOMIZE ON THEIR CANDLES, EVEN IF THEY HAD TO GROPE THEIR WAY OUT IN THE DARK...

BECKY, CAN YOU BEAR IT IF I TELL YOU SOMETHING?

I...I THINK I COULD, TOM!

WELL, THEN, BECKY, WE MUST STAY HERE WHERE THERES WATER TO DRINK! THAT LITTLE PIECE IS OUR LAST CANDLE!

BECKY GAVE LOOSE TO TEARS AND WAILING...

BOOOO! NOW, THEY'LL NEVER FIND US, AND WE'LL BOTH DIE IN THIS HORRIBLE CAVE!

PLEASE, BECKY, DON'T CRY! THEY'RE BOUND TO COME LOOKIN' FOR US WHEN THEY FIND OUT WE'RE MISSIN'!

SUDDENLY...

SH.!..DID YOU HEAR THAT?

I HEARD IT, TOM! IT SOUNDED LIKE A FAINT SHOUT!

H-O-O-O-O THERE! Y-O-O-O!

H-O-O-O-O THERE! Y-O-O-O-O!

HIS REPEATED SHOUTS BROUGHT NO ANSWER BUT THE MOCKING ECHO OF HIS OWN VOICE...

THE HEART-SINKING MISERY OF IT! TOM WHOOPED TILL HE WAS HOARSE, THEN AN IDEA STRUCK HIM...

I'LL TIE THIS KITE LINE HERE, SO WE CAN FIND OUR WAY BACK! COME ON, BECKY, WE'LL GO UP THIS PASSAGE!

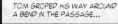

TOM GROPED HIS WAY AROUND A BEND IN THE PASSAGE...

SUDDENLY...

WHAT'S THIS -- OOOOO!

TOM, WHY DID YOU CRY OUT SO?

I-I GUESS I JUST SHOUTED FOR LUCK! COME, LET'S GET OUT OF HERE!

HE LED BECKY AS FAR AWAY FROM THE PASSAGE AS THEY COULD GO AND KISSED HER WITH A CHOKING SENSATION IN HIS THROAT...

FOR THREE DAYS, THE VILLAGE WAS STEEPED IN MOURNING FOR THE TWO LOST CHILDREN. MRS. THATCHER WAS VERY ILL AND AUNT POLLY HAD DROPPED INTO A SETTLED MELANCHOLY...

IN THE MIDDLE OF THE THIRD NIGHT, A WILD PEAL BURST FROM THE VILLAGE BELLS...

THE NEXT MOMENT...

TURN OUT! TURN OUT! THEY'RE FOUND!

TOM AND BECKY HAVE BEEN FOUND ALIVE!

HEAVEN BE PRAISED!

HERE THEY COME NOW! IT'LL BE GREAT NEWS FOR MRS. THATCHER!

AND FOR MRS. SAWYER, TOO! SHE'S WELL-NIGH CRIED HERSELF SICK!

SAFE AT HOME, TOM RELATED HIS WONDERFUL ADVENTURES, PUTTING IN MANY STRIKING ADDITIONS TO ADORN IT...

WELL, I STRUNG MY KITELINE THROUGH TWO OF THE PASSAGES, BUT HAD NO LUCK! THEN I TRIED A THIRD PASSAGE...

A LIGHT! HOORAY WE'RE SAVED!

I DROPPED MY LINE AND SHOVED ON IN THE DIRECTION OF THE LIGHT...

GOOD OLE MISSISSIPPI RIVER! WAIT'LL BECKY HEARS ABOUT THIS!

OH TOM, YOU MUST BE DELIRIOUS! I KNOW I'M GOING TO DIE HERE AND I DON'T CARE MUCH IF I DO!

BUT, BECKY, I SAW IT WITH MY OWN EYES! COME, I'LL SHOW YOU!

WE BOTH CLIMBED THROUGH THE HOLE AND I HAILED SOME MEN IN A SKIFF..

YOHO-O THERE!

THEN THEY TOOK US ABOARD, GAVE US SOMETHIN' TO EAT, AND THEN BROUGHT US HOME!

ABOUT A WEEK LATER, TOM WENT TO THE THATCHER HOUSE TO VISIT BECKY...

YOU KNOW, JUDGE THATCHER, I WOULDN'T MIND GOIN' BACK TO THAT CAVE AGAIN!

WELL, THERE ARE OTHERS LIKE YOU, TOM, BUT WE'VE TAKEN CARE OF THAT! NOBODY WILL GET LOST IN THAT CAVE ANYMORE!

WHY!

BECAUSE I HAD THE BIG DOOR SHEALTHED WITH BOILER IRON AND TRIPLE-LOCKED — AND I'VE GOT THE KEYS!

TOM TURNED AS WHITE AS A SHEET...

WHAT'S THE MATTER, BOY? HERE, RUN SOMEBODY FETCH A GLASS OF WATER!

THE WATER WAS BROUGHT AND THROWN INTO TOM'S FACE...

OH, JUDGE, INJUN JOE'S IN THE CAVE!

AN EXPEDITION WAS ORGANIZED AND INJUN JOE WAS FOUND IN THE CAVE, STARVED TO DEATH.

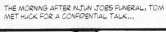
THE MORNING AFTER INJUN JOE'S FUNERAL, TOM MET HUCK FOR A CONFIDENTIAL TALK...

HUCK, I THINK I KNOW WHERE WE COULD FIND SOME BURIED TREASURE!

TOM, HONEST INJUN NOW, IS IT FOR FUN OR EARNEST?

JUST AS EARNEST AS I EVER WAS IN MY LIFE, I THINK INJUN JOE HAD A REASON FOR GOIN' TO THE CAVE AND IT WEREN'T JUST FOR A PLEASURE TRIP!

YOU MEAN INJUN JOE HAD A TREASURE BURIED IN THE CAVE?

SUREST THING, HUCK! I KNOW A SHORT CUT THAT'LL GET US TO THE SPOT IN A SKIFF!

JIMMINY, TOM! I DON'T SEE WHAT WE'RE WASTIN' TIME FOR! LET'S GO!

WE'LL TAKE ALONG A FEW KITE STRINGS, A PICK AND SOME AT THESE NEW-FANGLED MATCHES, I TELL YOU, MANY'S THE TIME I WISHT I HAD SOME WHEN I WAS IN THERE BEFORE!

THAT AFTERNOON...

NOW HUCK, WHERE WE'RE STANDING YOU COULD TOUCH THAT HOLE WE GOT OUT OF WITH A FISHIN'-POLE! SEE IF YOU CAN FIND IT!

HUCK SEARCHED THE PLACE THOROUGHLY AND FOUND NOTHING...

TOM PROUDLY MARCHED INTO A THICK CLUMP OF BUSHES...

HERE YOU ARE, HUCK! LOOK AT IT -- IT'S THE SNUGGEST HOLE IN THE COUNTRY!

IT SURE SOUNDS SPLENDID! WE'LL CALL IT TOM SAWYER'S GANG!

WE'LL GET JOE HARPER AND BEN ROGERS AND FORM A GANG!

WHY, IT'S REAL BULLY, HUCK! I BELIEVE IT'S BETTER'N BEIN' A PIRATE! IT'S CLOSER TO HOME AND CIRCUSES AN' ALL THAT!

SOON EVERYTHING WAS READY AND THE BOYS ENTERED THE HOLE...

YOU'RE SURE WE WON'T GET LOST, TOM?

SHUCKS! I KNOW MY WAY THROUGH HERE WITH MY EYES SHUT!

A FEW STEPS BROUGHT THEM TO THE SPRING...

GOSH!

YOU SEE THAT PIECE O' CANDLE ON THAT LEDGE, HUCK? BECKY AND I STOOD HERE AND WATCHED IT FLICKER AND THEN BURN OUT!

THEY WENT ON AND PRESENTLY REACHED ANOTHER CORRIDOR...

NOW I'LL SHOW YOU SOMETHING, HUCK!

THE CANDLE REVEALED A LARGE CROSS SMOKED ON THE ROCK...

IT'S A CROSS!

AND DONE WITH CANDLE SMOKE! HUCK, THIS IS THE VERY SPOT INJUN JOE WAS LAYIN' WITH A CANDLE IN HIS HAND!

THEN THIS IS THE SPOT WHERE HE BURIED THE TREASURE! COME ON, TOM, GET THAT PICK!

FOR A WHILE, THE PICK STRUCK NOTHING BUT SOLID ROCK, THEN...

I GOT THE SPOT, HUCK! THERES SOME SOFT CLAY HERE AND THE DIGGIN'S EASY!

HE HAD NOT DUG FOUR INCHES WHEN HE STRUCK WOOD...

HEY HUCK! YOU HEAR THAT?

SOUNDED LIKE WOOD! IT MUST BE THE TREASURE BOX!

BOY, OH BOY! THERE MUST BE A THOUSAND DOLLARS IN THAT CHEST!

MAYBE TWO THOUSAND OR THREE THOUSAND -- OR EVEN A MILLION!

HOORAY! WE'RE RICH!

YOOHOO! WE GOT IT! WE GOT THE TREASURE!

WHEN THE FIRST EXCITEMENT HAD SUBSIDED...

WHAT ARE YOU THINKIN' OF, TOM?

I WAS THINKIN' MAYBE WE SHOULDN'T OUGHTA GO IN FOR BEIN' ROBBERS! WITH ALL THAT MONEY, WE WON'T EVER HAVE TO GO TO SCHOOL AND WE COULD SPEND THE REST OF OUR LIVES JUST A' FISHIN'!

The End

Mark Twain
THE ADVENTURES OF
TOM SAWYER

The Adventures of Tom Sawyer has become the essential guidebook to American boyhood. Even though the world Tom occupies has gone the way of the buggy-whip, Tom's attitude remains in the heart of almost every child, but especially of every boy. He fights because he doesn't like another boy's hat. He runs away from home after being punished for something he didn't do. He steps forward to take someone else's punishment because that someone is a pretty girl. He can't get enough of books about buried treasure, digs for it himself, and in the end finds it.

Tom Sawyer is the best-remembered work of a wave of books from this era about scamps, rascals and trouble-makers. This flood, which began in 1869 with Thomas Bailey Aldrich's *The Story of a Bad Boy*, and continued for many years afterward, served a specific cultural purpose. In the wake of the Civil War, all of America was striving to find common ground again. Very few American writers of Twain's generation actually served on either side during the war, but they lived in a nation filled with veterans—with whom they did not share the central, important experience of war. To write about boys and boyhood was to take readers back to their own child-hood—to establish a common ground that had nothing to do with the civil war: 'after all, we were all boys once.'

Mark Twain's fellow literary great, William Dean Howells, read the manuscript of *Tom Sawyer* "sitting up till one A.M. to get to the end, simply because it was impossible to leave off," as he wrote his friend Samuel Langhorne Clemens, the man behind Twain. "It's altogether the best boy's story I have ever read." Howell's enthusiasm for the novel went hand-in-hand with his belief that the book was for children. He warned Twain that "if you should put it forth as a study of boy character from the grown-up point of view, you'd give the wrong key to it." Twain agreed, sensing that Tom Sawyer's charm lay not in his becoming a man but in his being a boy. "If I went on, now, & took him into manhood, he would be just like all the one-horse men in literature & the reader would conceive a hearty contempt for him." As he is, Tom Sawyer is the boy most men wish they'd had the courage to be.

Virginia City, Nevada, *Territorial Enterprise,* and—after adopting the pen name Mark Twain — became the best known of the new crop of all the Western writers.

By 1876, he had already made a fortune by writing, selling over 100,000 copies each of *Innocents Abroad* (1868), his knowing take on Europe, and *Roughing It* (1870), a broadly fictionalized retelling of his five years in the Wild West. He had also co-written a novel, *The Gilded Age* (1873), with Charles Dudley Warner, three years before *Tom Sawyer* was published. But when *The Gilded Age* came out, Mark Twain was considered merely a humorist; the book's political satire aroused more interest than its melodrama concerning the political intrigues of a ruined Southern woman.

Now, though, the 41-year-old Mark Twain had much more at stake. He had befriended William Dean Howells, the young editor of the taste-making *Atlantic Monthly*, and Howells championed Mark Twain's work with the literati of post-Civil War America. He had published "A True Story" (1874), a touching tale of a black woman's voyage out of slavery; "Old Times in the Mississippi" (1874-5), a series about how Sam Clemens became a pilot on the mighty river; and a great short story in

When Mark Twain wrote *The Adventures of Tom Sawyer,* the first novel he penned on his own, he was wildly anxious for its success. Born Samuel Langhorne Clemens in frontier Missouri in 1835, when Halley's comet was in the sky, he grew up in Hannibal, on the Mississippi. Like the other boys in town he wanted to become a riverboat pilot, but after a standard education, settled for joining his older brother in a printing and newspaper concern. At twenty-two he dropped out of the composing room and signed on as a pilot-trainee on a Mississippi steamboat, and soon became a pilot. The Civil War broke up the river trade, so in 1861 he accompanied his brother, recently named Secretary to the Nevada Territory, out West. After bumming around as a prospector for a few months, Sam took a job as a reporter on the which the narrator kills off his conscience, "The Facts Concerning the Recent Carnival of Crime in Connecticut" (1876). Despite these literary successes, most people still thought Mark Twain was more interested in selling *many* books than in writing *good* ones.

Tom Sawyer was Twain's first bid for real literary success, and he tried to control every aspect of the novel's publication. He got William Dean Howells to publish a thunderingly positive review of the book. "The story is a wonderful study of the boy-mind," Howells proclaimed, "which inhabits a world quite distinct from that in which he is bodily present with his elders, and in this lies its great charm and its universality, for boy nature, however human nature varies, is the same everywhere." Twain felt Howells' review would "embolden weak-kneed journalistic admirers to speak out, & will modify or shut up the unfriendly." He expected his publisher to release the novel just as this review appeared, but the publisher wasn't ready: the review promoted a book not yet for sale.

Also, in order to protect his British copyright, Twain tried to coordinate publication in England and America, while stirring up the publicity machine for both editions. The novel came out in England during the summer of 1876; within a month publishers in Canada were shipping cheap copies into the United States. Mark Twain's promotional efforts worked to sell thousands of pirate copies of *Tom Sawyer* for which he would not get a cent—so many copies that Clemens had to print up cards promising a sequel to the novel to answer all the mail he got requesting further adventures for Tom. When Mark Twain's publisher finally brought the novel to market in December, he sold only 25,000 copies, about a quarter of what Twain's other books had sold.

The financial debacle of *Tom Sawyer* led to a number of changes in Samuel Clemens's life. To save the money it cost to keep his mansion in Hartford, Connecticut, he took his family, including his heiress wife and two young daughters, to Europe for almost two years. He wrote another travel book about his stay, *A Tramp Abroad* (1879), which, combined with improvements in his wife Livy's finances, allowed them to return to

their lavish life. He wrote another book for children, *The Prince and the Pauper* (1881), which sold about as well as *Tom Sawyer* had, but which produced much more money, since Clemens had decided to become his own publisher. Another travel book, *Life on the Mississippi* (1882) expanded from his *Atlantic* series on piloting, sold very well, as did the sequel to Tom's story, *Adventures of Huckleberry Finn* (1884). His publishing firm then released the best-selling book of 19th century America, *The Personal Memoirs of Ulysses S. Grant*, the former President and victorious Civil War general.

Sam Clemens's fortune seemed made, until his nephew-by-marriage Charles L. Webster squandered the holdings of the publishing company, and Sam Clemens himself began investing every spare penny in a mechanical typesetter. He published only *A Connecticut Yankee in King Arthur's Court* (1889), his first novel intended for adults, before his finances failed in 1891. The family again left for Europe while the publishing company and his investment in the typesetter went through their death throes. In 1895-6, Sam Clemens took Mark Twain in a 'round the world lecture

> Tom Sawyer was Twain's first bid for real literary success, and he tried to control every aspect of the novel's publication

tour which earned back most of the money he owed; his book about the tour, *Following the Equator* (1897) put him back on the road to wealth. The family stayed on in Europe until 1900, when Twain returned to America, a homey philosopher doling wisdom, morality and forthrightness to every reporter who asked his opinion. He quickly became the country's most quoted and photographed citizen.

Clemens's return to solvency was no protection against grief, however. His eldest daughter Susy died of meningitis just before she was to sail to meet her father in England at the end of his world tour. Wife Livy never recovered from Susy's death, and she began a long decline which ended with her death in Florence in 1904. In the wake of her passing, Clemens drank too much, fell under the influence of his secretary, started a series of ambiguous relationships with teenage girls, and quarreled with his two surviving daughters, Clara and Jean. Clara, fearful that the secretary would marry her father and squander his fortune, began a campaign against her. Clara's accusations eventually proved true, and Clara and Jean returned to their father's household. In the fall of 1909 Clara married; a few months later, just before Christmas, Jean, who was epileptic, had a seizure while bathing and drowned. Alone now, Samuel Clemens died the following spring, in April 1910; Halley's comet was in the sky.

CONTEXT: BRET HARTE

Bret Harte was the most successful writer in post-Civil War San Francisco. Mark Twain had more success in publishing back East, but Bret Harte was the founder and editor of *The Californian*, a Bohemian with a post at the San Francisco Mint, and the major literary taste-setter for the West Coast. As a young writer, Sam Clemens allowed Bret Harte to dictate his literary style, and submitted *Innocents Abroad* to his extensive editing. When Harte hit it big in the East three years after Mark Twain, landing an *Atlantic* contract paying $10,000 for a year of monthly contributions, Clemens was jealous and angry. He had yet to have a story accepted by *The Atlantic*; four years later, when he finally did, he received only $60 for it.

But Bret Harte's star burned out quickly. He borrowed money he didn't repay, drank heavily, and failed to complete his contracts. When Sam Clemens stepped in to "save" him, he had no goodwill left for his old mentor. They co-wrote a play; then Mark Twain squeezed him out of the production. Sam got his own publisher to buy Bret Harte's novel *Gabriel Conroy*, then let *Tom Sawyer* run in direct competition with it so he could out-sell the man who had once bested him. Mark Twain harbored a grudge against Bret Harte for more than twenty years.

THE CHARACTERS

Tom Sawyer: a boy of uncertain age, mother dead, father unknown

Aunt Polly: sister to Tom's mother, raising Tom and

Sid: Tom's younger half-brother, with

Mary: Tom's and Sid's cousin, Aunt Polly's daughter

Jim: the family's African-American boy, possibly a slave

Mr. Dobbins: Tom's school teacher

Mr. Walters: the Sunday School superintendent

Joe Harper: Tom's closest friend

Alfred Temple: Tom's sworn enemy

Ben Rogers, Billy Fisher, Johnny Miller, Jeff Thatcher: friends of Tom's

Lawyer Thatcher: Jeff's father, a near neighbor of Tom's family

Judge Thatcher: the lawyer's brother, from the nearby town of Constantinople

Becky Thatcher: the Judge's daughter, Tom's new love interest

Amy Lawrence: Tom's old love interest

Huckleberry Finn: neglected son of the town drunk

Muff Potter: another town drunk

Injun Joe: a murdering thief, half Native American, other half unknown

The Widow Douglas: a kindly well-to-do woman on whom Injun Joe has sworn revenge

Dr. Robinson: the town's young physician, murdered in the process of grave robbing.

PLOT ANALYSIS

The Adventures of Tom Sawyer opens with the orphan Tom's Aunt Polly searching everywhere for her misbehaving nephew. Grabbing him just as he's about to escape from his hiding place (p. 3 panel 2) she makes ready to whip him, until Tom distracts her and he runs. Aunt Polly only laughs (p. 3 panel 5) in a way that cues the readers into how we should feel about young Tom Sawyer: "He's full of the Old Scratch"—the devil— "but laws-a-me! he's my own dead sister's boy, poor thing, and I ain't got the heart to lash him." Tom, of a deliberately uncertain but pre-adolescent age, is more high-spirited than evil-minded. He is also completely devoted to romantic tales about robbers, Indians and pirates, and bases his entire existence on what he takes to be the rules of life as embodied in these books. The rules set down by his Aunt Polly, his teacher Mr. Dobbins or the Sunday School superintendent Mr. Walters are mere annoyances. Breaking those rules may lead to a whipping but, as Tom says, "Who cares for that?" He follows a higher law: he must do whatever leads him to greater adventure and more respect from the other boys in the town, and from whatever girl he has chosen to idolize.

Playing hooky and engaging in a pointless fight with a new boy in town lands him the job of whitewashing his Aunt's fence (chapter 2) At first he's desperate to escape from the labor—he is smart enough to know that he can't just walk away from the task—but then he realizes that he can trick his friends into trading their valuables for the chance to whitewash by pretending it is the most exciting thing any boy anywhere could do (pp. 10-12). By mid-afternoon, the fence is whitewashed and he's rich. Then he trades all his new wealth for the tickets pupils earn for learning Bible verses, accumulating enough tickets to win a new

Bible, an accomplishment legitimately accomplished only by the oldest scholars in Sunday School. The goal isn't just to get out of painting the fence, and it certainly isn't to get a Bible. Tom Sawyer only wants to make himself conspicuous in St. Petersburg.

Tom has friends, like Joe Harper and Ben Rogers, but there is one person whose company Tom most desires, "the juvenile pariah of the village, Huckleberry Finn." The mothers in the town all despise Huck "because all their children admired him so, and delighted in his forbidden society, and wished they dared to be like him." Tom treasures Huck not only because he sleeps in barrels, wears men's old cast-off clothes and answers to no one, but also because he has less social standing than the orphan Tom. As long as Tom behaves better than Huck, he never has to try to be as good as his prissy half-brother Sid (chapter 4). On his

Themes: Love, Livy Langdon, and Becky Thatcher

The Adventures of Tom Sawyer had its origins in Sam Clemens's courtship of Olivia Langdon. Langdon, the daughter of a successful upstate New York coal merchant, had been a sickly teenager, and spent several years alone in a New York City clinic recovering from Pott's Disease, tuberculosis of the spine. Clemens was 32 when he met her through her younger brother in late December, 1867, and Livy was 22, quiet and somber. Eight months later he traveled to her home in Elmira. He stayed in the Langdon mansion for two weeks and, after this very brief acquaintance, asked Livy's father, Jervis, for permission to court her. In uncertain health and worried about his girl, Jervis Langdon agreed.

Clemens immediately proposed. Livy declined, but did tell him he could write her as though her were her brother. This was a code to say that Livy accepted being courted without accepting the proposal. Since she was without other suitors, it could also be taken to mean that she would accept a proposal of marriage at another time, when they knew each other better. Clemens did not understand these upper-class rituals, and worried himself sick about the courtship. After a few weeks, however, he began to understand that he *had* to go through these odd social hoops to win his wealthy bride, a performance not unlike what he remembered from boyhood, when he tried to catch the heart of a girl by showing off, while both pretended neither knew the other was nearby. To vent his fustration, he wrote a savage burlesque of this weird mating dance. Almost ten years later he pulled it out of the drawer, sweetened the tone, and put it into *Tom Sawyer*.

way to school, he meets up with Huck, who wants to try out a cure for warts that involves a dead cat and a cemetery at midnight. When Tom shows up late to school, he confesses to fraternizing with the pariah to get other boys' respect, as well as to get the chance to sit beside his new crush, Becky Thatcher, to whom he confesses his love. The plot of the book meanders until these two confessions come together, bringing Tom's enthusiasm for adventure together with the romantic mysteries of love.

Near midnight, Huck meows for Tom, who climbs out his window. The boys make their way to the graveyard, where they find they are not alone. (Chapter 9). The young Dr. Robinson wants a cadaver and

has hired the drunk, Muff Potter, and the vile Injun Joe to dig up a fresh corpse. The deal goes wrong: The doctor strikes Injun Joe; Potter defends his friend. When the doctor knocks out Potter, Injun Joe stabs the doctor in the heart (p. 27 panels 3 and 4). Tom and Huck scamper, agreeing not to tell anyone anything of what they have seen. Injun Joe tells the law that Muff Potter is the murderer, and Potter, too drunk to know whether he is or not, surrenders to the law.

Tom's life becomes a misery. The boys in town constantly play out the murder and the inquest, but Tom fears he'll let slip that he knew what happened, and thus dares not join in. Becky Thatcher discovers that Tom had loved Amy Lawrence before her, and now refuses to speak to him. His listlessness concerns his Aunt Polly, who tries all manner of potions and cures to revive his spirits. After a public rebuke from Becky, Tom "was gloomy and desperate. He was a forsaken, friendless boy, he said, nobody loved him; when they found out what they had driven him to, perhaps they would be sorry; he had tried to do right and get along, but they would not let him." He decides to abandon society and take to a life of crime.

No sooner does Tom make this decision than he finds Joe Harper, filled with the same determination. The two, together with Huck Finn, snag some food and a wooden raft and push off across the Mississippi to an uninhabited island (p. 29 panel 1), where they set up as pirates, sleeping on the ground, scratching their food out of the river, learning to smoke, subjecting themselves to no one's rule.

Of course, Joe's and Tom's families soon miss them, and a search party is called. Searchers fire a cannon over the surface in the belief that the sound will make the boys bodies rise to the surface. Hidden on the island, Tom, Joe and Huck realize they've been missed and are presumed dead.

Though at first "jubilant with vanity over their new grandeur and the harum-scarum, you know." He stays until the house falls quiet, creeps to his Aunt's bed with his note—then returns the note to his pocket and leaves only a kiss. He has an idea!

Back on the island the other pirates have begun to tire of their games. Tom can only get them to stay on by telling his idea: the church will hold a funeral for them on Sunday, and if they can

illustrious trouble they were making," Tom and Joe "could not keep back thought of certain persons back home who were not enjoying this fine frolic as much as they were." Tom lets Joe suggest going home first, and then "withered him with derision" Joe is "glad to get out of the scrape with as little taint of chicken-hearted homesickness clinging to his garments as he could." Once his comrades fall asleep, however, Tom hastens back home, just to leave his Aunt a note to assuage her worry. He sneaks into the house and overhears Joe's mother and Aunt Polly commiserate with Tom's half-brother Sid and cousin Mary: Tom "warn't bad, so to say—only *mischeevous*. Only just giddy and

hold out until then, the three can sneak into town on Saturday night, hide in the church, and attend their own memorial services. Huck and Joe agree (chapter 14) and, in the middle of the sermon, "the congregation rose and stared while the three dead boys came marching up the aisle, Tom in the lead, Joe next, and Huck, a ruin of drooping rags, sneaking sheepishly in the rear!" (p. 31 panel 5). The families "threw themselves upon their restored ones, smothered them with kisses and poured out thanksgiving." Unloved Huck starts to "slink away, but Tom seized him and said "'Aunt Polly, it ain't fair. Somebody's got to be glad to see Huck.'" Aunt Polly showers Huck with an embarrassment of affection, but alternates hugs and cuffs for Tom, until she discovers in his jacket pocket the affectionate note he decided not to leave for her.

Despite his vacation on the island and his improved status after his return, Tom finds his life more or less just as he left it. Becky still won't talk to him; school drags on toward summer; Muff Potter is still in jail awaiting trial, and the secret of the murder still weighs heavily on Tom. He tries to resolve these problems, with varying success. He flirts openly with Amy Lawrence, but Becky responds first by inviting everyone but Tom and Amy to a picnic, and then by flirting with Alfred Temple, the good boy Tom thrashes at the beginning of the book. When Tom appears unmoved, Becky casts Alfred aside; he takes his revenge by pouring ink on Tom's spelling book, an act Becky sees but does not report. Not long after, Tom catches Becky sneaking a look at the teacher's prized and secret book on human anatomy; she accidentally rips an illustration, then begs Tom not to tell on her.

Context Race and in Mark Twain's World

One of the ways Mark Twain made *The Adventures of Tom Sawyer* suitable for children was to squelch most references to race. Jim, the "small colored boy" who seems to work for Aunt Polly, is never referred to as a slave, although he calls Tom "Mars Tom," and refers to Aunt Polly as "Ole Missis." Another African-American makes a brief appearance: Ben Roger's "pap's nigger man, Uncle Jake. I tote water for Uncle Jake whenever he wants me to," Huck explains. "That's a mighty good nigger, Tom. He likes me, becuz I don't ever act as if I was above him." (Still, Huck doesn't want it spread around that he sometimes eats with Uncle Jake.) On the other hand, the only source of evil in the book is Injun Joe, about whom Huck says, "that murderin' half-breed! I'd druther they was devils, a dern sight."

Samuel Clemens was only just developing an egalitarian sensibility when he wrote *Tom Sawyer*. A child of the South, he developed strong prejudices about Blacks and Indians, ideas which he later worked hard to overcome. Within a few years of publication of this novel, Mark Twain was known as one of the nation's most forward-thinking people on the issue of race. Even so, he believed that people showed gradations of savagery, indicated by their cleanliness and their treatment of women. As he once remarked, "I can stand any society. All that I care to know is that a man is a human being—that is enough for me; he can't be any worse."

He agrees, but she still resists telling Tom what she knows about the ink on his book. The schoolmaster soon discovers the soiled spelling book and whips Tom for it. An hour passes before Dobbins finds the torn anatomy illustration, but before Becky can confess, Tom takes the blame. (chapter 21). Becky, new admiration blossoming in her eyes, sighs: "Tom, how could you be so noble!"

Then Tom goes through a series of scrapes. School draws to a close with a ceremony Tom makes unforgettable in a complex scheme to humiliate Mr. Dobbins, the teacher. One of Tom's friends lowers a muffled kitten above the master's head; the poor cat snatches Dobbins's toupee, revealing his bald head, painted a bright gold by Tom's allies. Tom joins the Cadets of Temperance just for the uniform he'd get to wear in a

QUICK AS LIGHTNING, THE HALF-BREED SPRANG FOR A WINDOW AND WAS GONE...

parade, but quits before he gets to wear it. He falls ill and recovers, only to find that all his friends have gotten religion and don't want to play, only pray. He has a relapse and, when he's better, finds that all his friends have had relapses too. The boys play at minstrel shows, pirates, war, and circus.

But Tom and Huck have more serious business: visiting Muff Potter in jail as the trial begins. "Tom went home miserable, and his dreams that night were full of horrors." The next day and the day after, he hung about the court room, drawn by an almost irresistible impulse to go in, but forcing himself to stay out. Huck had the same experience." In the end, Tom's conscience wins out. (chapter 24). He secretly tells Potter's lawyer what he saw in the cemetery, and the next day testifies in court. Before anyone in the court can apprehend him, Injun Joe disappears (p. 34 panel 2).

"Tom was the glittering hero once more," but "his nights were seasons of horror." He worries that Injun Joe will come back to slit his throat. "Since Tom's harassed conscience had managed to drive him to the lawyer's house by night and wring a dread tale from lips that had been sealed with the dismalest and most formidable of oaths, Huck's confidence in the human race was well nigh obliterated. Daily Muff Potter's gratitude made Tom glad he had spoken; but nightly he wished he had sealed up his tongue." Tom believes he'll never rest easy until Injun Joe is dead.

But boys have short memories. Before long, Tom and Huck decide to go treasure hunting because "There comes a time in every rightly constructed boy's life when he has a raging desire to go somewhere and dig for hidden treasure." At first Tom and Huck dig during the day, but they soon realize they won't have any luck unless they dig where the moon throws a certain shadow at midnight. When even that fails, they tempt fate by going into an abandoned house to

Themes: The Cave

The cave in *The Adventures of Tom Sawyer* actually exists just outside of Hannibal, Missouri; it is a tremendously dangerous maze cut by nature into the rock beneath the ground. Mark Twain noted in the novel that "No man 'knew' the cave. That was an impossible thing. Most of the young men knew a portion of it, and it was not customary to venture beyond this known portion. Tom Sawyer"—Sam Clemens, that is— "knew as much of the cave as anyone." Called McDowell's Cave for the physician who owned the land above it, the cave was the place Hannibal's young people went when they wanted respite from their close chaperonage.

Dr. McDowell, who founded a medical school in St. Louis, had another plan for the cave. He had hung a glass-lined copper cylinder containing the corpse of a teenage girl in an alcohol solution in one of the cave's recesses. He wanted to see if the cave would reduce the corpse to bones, so that he could turn the property into a mausoleum. Hannibal's boys, however, used to go to the cave to sneak a look at the naked dead girl; Sam Clemens was probably one of the girl's regular visitors. With the mix of danger and secrecy, the cave always seemed to Clemens a nexus of sex and death.

look for treasure. While they are there, two strangers show up, and the boys hide upstairs. One of the strangers turns out to be Injun Joe in disguise; (chapter 27) he has been using the haunted house as his hideout. He and his partner have come to plan their last criminal escapade before leaving for Texas. As they dig a hole to hide their loot, they discover just what the boys have been looking for, thousands of dollars in gold, left behind by another, more successful band of robbers. Injun Joe takes the gold with him to hide in his den—"Number Two— under the cross." Huck and Tom, distraught at losing a fortune, agree to follow, find Injun Joe's hideaway, and capture the gold.

Their hunt is interrupted by Becky Thatcher's long-delayed picnic. Leaving Huck as guard, Tom joins the large crowd of children down river where, after the banquet and some outdoor fun, the group goes into McDougal's cave, a winding labyrinth of connecting passages twisting deep beneath the earth. Tom and Becky purposely separate themselves from the others to get a little private time. They take a turn down a previously unexplored passageway hidden behind a rock formation that looks like a frozen waterfall, (chapter 30) and before long are frightened by a mass of bats. Scampering away, they lose the rodents but also lose their way. They are trapped in the cave.

Meanwhile, Huck follows Injun Joe and his partner, who have a plan to rob the Widow Douglas. The Widow's husband once had Injun Joe horsewhipped in front of the whole town, and he wants revenge. "When you want revenge in a woman," he tells his partner, "You go for her looks. You slit her nostrils—you notch her ears, like a sow's." Huck has heard enough. He runs to get help, but he doesn't wait around to find out the result. The next morning he finds that the Widow Douglas has escaped injury, but that the two criminals have escaped. Injun Joe is still on the loose.

The thwarted attack is the talk of the town the next morning, but soon another topic replaces it: Tom and Becky are still missing. Again, the town organizes a search party for Tom Sawyer and his friends, but the cave is so deep and complex, no one has much hope of finding the two children alive.

In the cave, Tom and Becky have wandered for hour after hour, slowly picking their way through the dark using a kite string to assure their return to a place where there is water. When Becky can explore no further, Tom continues alone. (chapter 32) On one foray, he sees a candle light and a hand. He lets out a shout; at the sound a figure—Injun Joe's—scurries away. Tom doesn't know whether to be despondent or relieved. After a long sleep, Tom and Becky awake famished and desperate. Becky refuses to go on; Tom refuses to stop. He follows the kite string to its very end, "and was about to turn back when he glimpsed a far-off speck that looked like daylight; dropped the line and groped toward it, pushed his head and shoulders through a small hole and saw the

broad Mississippi rolling by!" The exit to safety is nearly five miles further away from St. Petersburg. It is Tuesday night before Tom and Becky return to town, by which time most of the searchers have given up.

Tom and Becky slowly recover—Tom's recovery speeded by news of the shoot-out near the Widow Douglas's and the discovery of the drowned body of Injun Joe's partner. Eventually Tom goes to visit Becky and finds a crowd at the Judge's house. "Someone asked him ironically if he wouldn't like to go to the cave again. Tom said yes, he thought he wouldn't mind it." But the Judge has sealed off and triple-locked the cave mouth. Tom is horrified at the news, and manages to splutter, (chapter 33) "'Oh, Judge, Injun Joe's in the cave" (p. 40 bottom left). A dozen skiffloads of men head to the cave. The Judge unlocks the door to reveal the corpse of Injun Joe, starved to death. "Injun Joe was buried near the mouth of the cave; and people flocked there in boats and wagons from the town and from all the farms and hamlets for seven miles around; they brought their children, and all sorts of provisions, and confessed that they had almost as satisfactory a time at the funeral as they could have had at the hanging." For everyone but Huck and Tom, the story is at a close.

For the two boys, there is still treasure to be found. Tom persuades Huck to go with him; he feels certain the treasure is in the cave, in the very portion where he and Becky were lost, where he had last seen the murderer alive. They could go in by the very passage through which Tom saved himself and Becky. Huck is reluctant, but Tom entices him with a plan to form a band of robbers, kidnapping people for the ransom. Robbers hold the people they kidnap for a year and "then you kill them. That's the general way. Only you don't kill the women. You shut up the women, but you don't kill them. They're always beautiful and rich and awfully scared." Huck is all for it. Once in the cave, the boys find another warren of rooms Injun Joe had marked with a cross: there they find the money, $12,000 worth.

They drag the fortune back to town, where they find themselves the toast of a surprise party. (chapter 35) The reason: Tom's pesky half-brother Sid has revealed Huck's role in saving the Widow Douglas. But though Sid has ruined one secret, Tom has another,

better one: the treasure. Huck and Tom are now both rich, with fortunes that earn them each a dollar a day: "a dollar and a quarter a week would board, lodge and school a boy in those simple days—and clothe him and wash him, too, for that matter."

Of course, Huck hates being washed and clothed and schooled, but the Widow Douglas takes him in as her own and insists. He runs off, but Tom tracks him down telling him he can't be a robber if he's a bum. "In most countries they're awful high up in the nobility—dukes and such." Huck agrees to "stick with the widder till I rot, Tom; and if I git to be a reglar ripper of a robber, and everybody talking 'bout it, I reckon she'll be proud she snaked me in out of the wet." Judge Thatcher, meanwhile, "conceived a great opinion of Tom" and said "he meant to look to it that Tom should be admitted to the National military academy and afterward trained in the best law school in the country." Tom's fortune is made.

Context: *Tom Sawyer*, after *Tom Sawyer*

The Adventures of Tom Sawyer was only the first of many books Mark Twain wrote featuring Tom. He figures prominently in *Adventures of Huckleberry Finn* and became the lead character in several books and stories written for children, though most went unpublished. *Tom Sawyer, Detective* and *Tom Sawyer Among the Indians* are available in paperback. *Tom Sawyer Abroad* was the first in a projected series covering all the countries of the globe. In all these books, Tom is still a boy. But when Clemens returned to Missouri in 1902 to receive an honorary degree, he visited Hannibal for the last time and came away with the idea of writing the story of the two old friends, Tom and Huck, returning to *their* home town fifty years later. Most of their old gang is dead by now, and Tom and Huck, withered like the rest, die in one another's arms. Of the many manuscripts Clemens chose not to publish in his lifetime, this is the only one he seemingly destroyed.

• Mark Twain notes in the preface that "Huck Finn is drawn from life;" in fact, Clemens's sister immediately recognized him as Tom Blankenship, a boy a few years older than Sam Clemens, who lived with his large and slovenly family in a ramshackle barn of a house a stone's throw from where Clemens spent most of his Hannibal years. He also claims that Tom Sawyer "is a combination of the characteristics of three boys whom I knew, and therefore belongs to the composite order of architecture." Tom's family, however, is drawn from Clemens's own: Mary is like his sister Mela; Sid like his brother Henry, and Aunt Polly like his mother Jane. Why does Clemens deny that he was the model for Tom Sawyer?

• What role does class play in the novel? Can you graph the hierarchy of classes in Hannibal society and describe their relationships?

• *The Adventures of Tom Sawyer* has long been criticized as a book which only boys can enjoy. Is it? How are boys and girls likely to read it differently? How are men and women likely to read it differently? What difference does the age of the reader, of either sex, make?

• Why did Tom testify against Injun Joe? Yes, it was the right thing to do, but Tom doesn't often do the right thing unless he has something more material to gain than merely feeling virtuous. What else did Tom have to gain?

• The novel is so filled with folk superstitions that folklorists have long used it as evidence of what people thought in the Missouri backwoods during the Jacksonian era. Other than providing local color, what role do superstitions play in the novel? What is the relationship between folk beliefs and the rules of behavior Tom learns from his cheap novels? Which set of beliefs has more authority in the course of *Tom Sawyer*?

• Why do the twin climaxes of the novel—Tom's rescue of Becky, and Tom's discovery of the money—take place in the cave? What does the cave represent?

• Tom Sawyer seems to have a peculiar value system in which questions of good and evil play less of

a role than questions of popularity and greed. Is Tom morally corrupt? Why?

• Why does Mark Twain take up thirty pages in the middle of the novel with the boys' escape to the island? What purpose does the diversion serve, if any?

• Why did Mark Twain call Tom Sawyer's town St. Petersburg? What is the connection between this place and St. Peter?

• Why does the novel include all the material about the relationship between Tom Sawyer and Becky Thatcher? How do their romantic fluctuations fit in with the rest of the action of the novel, which includes grave robbing, murder, buried treasure, mistaken identity, and runaway boys?

• The first several chapters of the novel cover Tom's life almost minute by minute, but the pace of events speeds up considerably until the end. Is this purposeful? If it isn't, what is the point? Is it a flaw in the novel? If so, how does this odd pacing hamper the book?

• In your view, what is the book's best, most enduring characteristic? Is this why it has become a classic? Do you think it deserves to be considered a classic? Why? Why not?

ABOUT THE ESSAYIST:

Andrew Jay Hoffman is the author of Inventing Mark Twain, a biography of Samuel Langhorne Clemens; Beehive: a novel; and Twain's Heroes, Twain's Worlds. A Visiting Scholar at Brown University, he holds a Ph. D. in Literature from Brown University.